BARRY
THE FISH WITH FINGERS

For the Barry
who is not a fish

SIMON & SCHUSTER
First published in the UK in 2009
This edition first published in 2019
by Simon & Schuster UK Ltd
1st Floor, 222 Gray's Inn Road, London, WC1X 8HB
A CBS Company

A CIP catalogue record for this book is available
from the British Library upon request

ISBN: 978-1-4711-7818-4 (PB) • 978-0-8570-7397-6 (eBook)

Printed in China

3 5 7 9 10 8 6 4 2

BARRY

THE FISH WITH FINGERS

by Sue Hendra
and Paul Linnet

SIMON & SCHUSTER
London New York Sydney Toronto New Delhi

Puffy, the puffer fish, could blow the BEST bubbles. Other fish would come from miles around to see his bubble-blowing show.

Big bubbles, small bubbles, round bubbles, square bubbles – they had never seen anything quite so amazing until . . .

They caught sight of Barry.

Barry was no ordinary fish.

Barry was a fish with fingers!

Suddenly, everyone wanted to find out more about the amazing fish with fingers.

"What can your fingers do, Barry?" they asked. "Tell us, tell us!"

"Well," said Barry. "Fingers mean . . ."

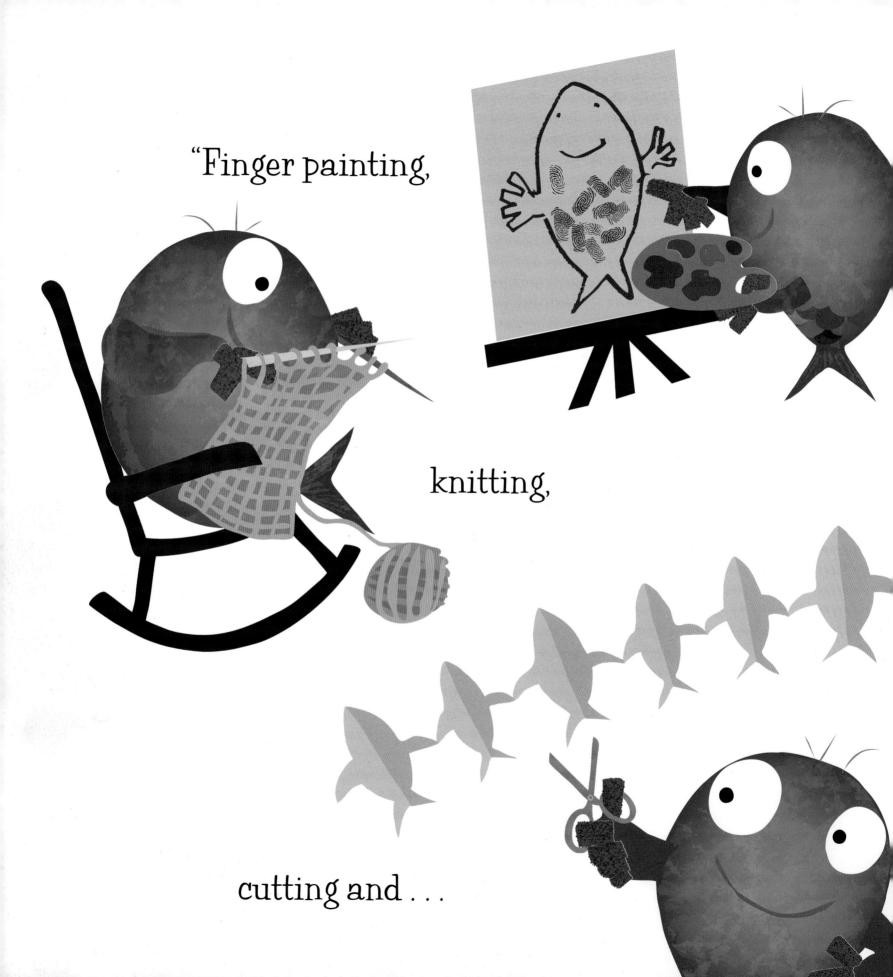

"Finger painting,

knitting,

cutting and . . .

FINGER PUPPETS!

But, best of all,
fingers mean ..."

The fish had never had so much fun.
"Come on, Puffy. Join in!" said Barry.

But Puffy didn't want to join in.
He was feeling sad.

"Now nobody wants to see my bubble-blowing show,"
he sighed. "I hate Barry's fingers. They're stupid!"

So while Puffy sulked on his own, Barry and the other fish had a whale of a time, chasing each other through sea caves, in and out of seashells and through the seaweed.

But, all of a sudden, Barry stopped dead in his tracks.

He heard a loud splash and a rumbling noise.

Then the sea got darker and a big shadow covered the ocean. "Oh, no!" cried Barry.

"Oh, no!" cried the fish.
A huge crate had fallen into the water
and it was going to squash Puffy.

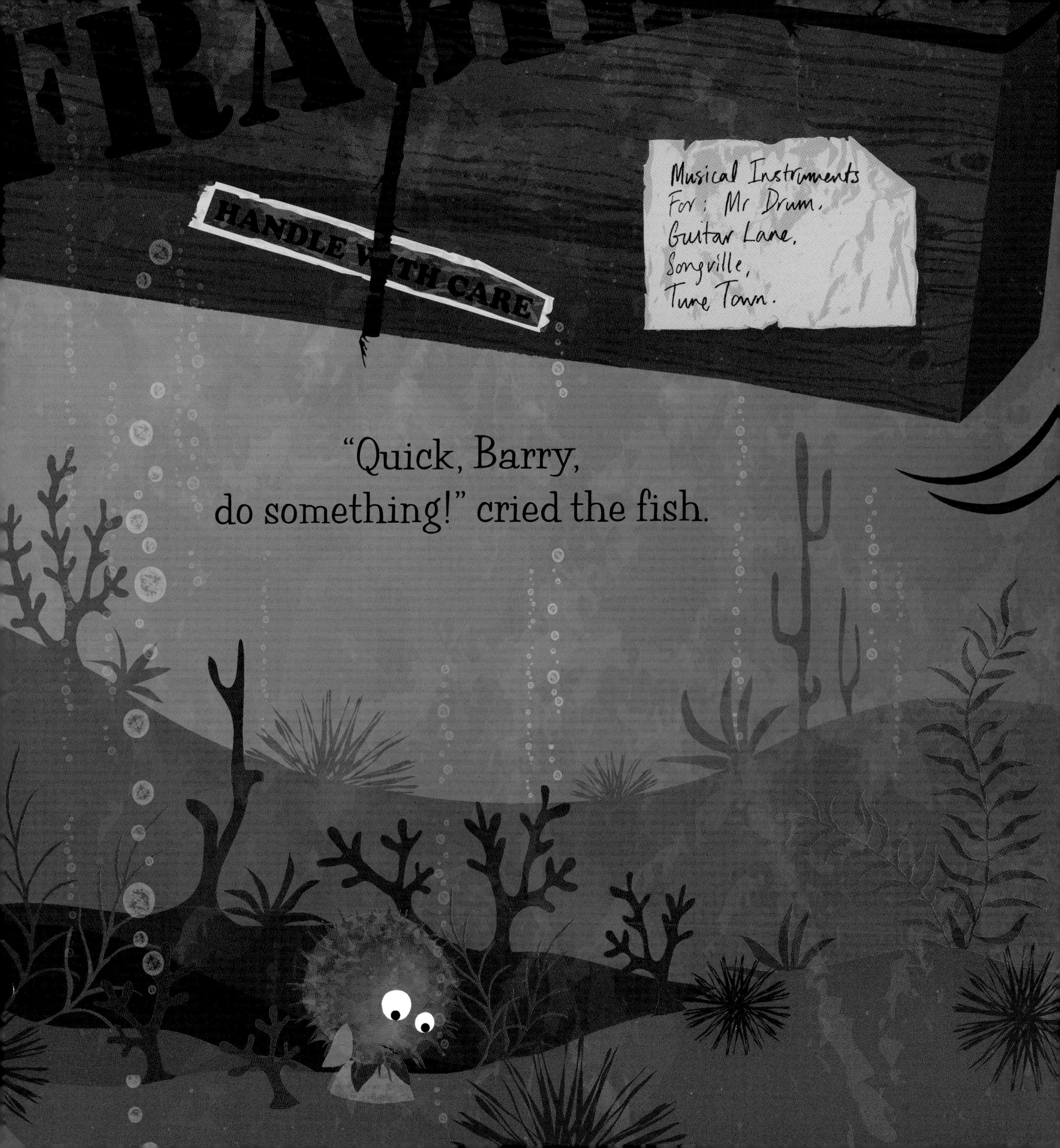

HANDLE WITH CARE

Musical Instruments
For: Mr Drum,
Guitar Lane,
Songville,
Tune Town.

"Quick, Barry,
do something!" cried the fish.

And that was when Barry did something truly amazing –

he pointed!
"Look out, Puffy!"

With a loud

CRASH!

the crate hit the sea bed.

Was it too late?
Had poor Puffy been squashed?

Musical Instruments
For Mr Drum.
Guitar Lane.
Songville,
Tune Town.

Phew!
No, he hadn't.

"Thank you, Barry," said Puffy. "You saved my life. I'm sorry for being a grumpy spoilsport. Can we play tickle chase?"

But Barry had a better idea . . .

"LET'S PARTY!"

"Take it away, Puffy!" he cried.
So Barry played the piano, Puffy blew the trumpet
and everyone had the BEST time ever.

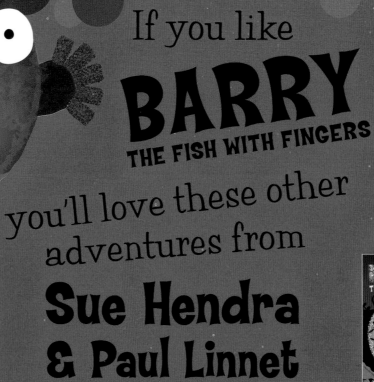

If you like

BARRY
THE FISH WITH FINGERS

you'll love these other adventures from

Sue Hendra
& Paul Linnet

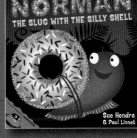

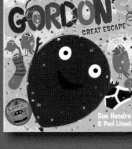

BARRY
THE FISH WITH FINGERS
AND THE HAIRY SCARY MONSTER
Sue Hendra
& Paul Linnet

NORMAN
THE SLUG WITH THE SILLY SHELL
Sue Hendra
& Paul Linnet

DOUG
Sue Hendra
& Paul Linnet

NO-BOT
THE ROBOT WITH NO BOTTOM!
SUE HENDRA
& PAUL LINNET

NORMAN
THE SLUG WHO SAVED CHRISTMAS
Sue Hendra
& Paul Linnet

GORDON
GREAT ESCAPE
Sue Hendra
& Paul Linnet

KEITH
THE CAT WITH THE MAGIC HAT
Sue Hendra
& Paul Linnet

WEE!

SUPERTATO
Sue Hendra
& Paul Linnet

SUPERTATO
VEGGIES ASSEMBLE
Sue Hendra
& Paul Linnet

SUPERTATO
RUN, VEGGIES, RUN!
Sue Hendra
& Paul Linnet

SUPERTATO
EVIL PEA RULES!
Sue Hendra
& Paul Linnet

SUPERTATO
VEGGIES IN THE VALLEY OF DOOM
Sue Hendra
& Paul Linnet